THE STORY OF HER

Zachary Ross

Bere Wildness Productions

*For HER,
and
all we were and could have ever hoped to be...*

"My affections and wishes are unchanged; but one word from you will silence me on this subject for ever."

PRIDE & PREJUDICE BY JANE AUSTEN

PROLOGUE

My heart yearns for something or someone. They're one and the same if I'm really being honest. Either way, I don't need 'em for long. Just long enough to keep me booked, busy and entertained until something more interesting comes along and snatches my attention.

What can I say? I love the thrill of awakening them for a few months, with no real intention to see it through. But who knows? This next time might be different, or it might not. Doesn't matter, really. I'll figure it out along the way. For now, it's an easy one-two. I'll just do what I always do: I will enter her life embodying everything that she admires, then, I will be her demise, as I leave her for something better.

Hmmm...Hello. She's a pretty little thing, isn't she? Another conquest? Oh? Another challenge. Yes, you're who I choose. Someone I can corrupt. Conquer. Crush. Because you're already taken, but again, it doesn't matter.
I will have HER.

FOR HER,

and

all we were and could have ever hoped to be...

1

I'm not able to convey this to you face-to-face and being who I am, I find it easier to tell you like this so the rejection that will follow isn't as harsh as I think it will be, and I can be as animated as possible...

※ ※ ※

It's always those introductions in a class where you're asked to say your name and expectations for whatever course you're doing that you realize the hidden gems in the room. As they rise to fulfil the lecturer's irritating requirement, you sit at the edge of your seat anxious for them to be unveiled, dreading your own turn. YOU did not disappoint me.

Your sweet soft voice travelled across the tense classroom void, as you went through the motions written on the board. Although this was not my first time seeing you, it was my first time hearing your voice, and I can say with one-hundred percent affirmation that I was completely and wholeheartedly smitten! I guess that must come as a shock and have you wondering why I chose you... maybe? Or how someone like you, who did not want to be seen, was able to demand my attention with just a few measly words?

The Mandeville weather was being its usual bipolar self: warm, sunny, beach weather one minute, then a devastating hurricane-like thunderstorm in no less than twenty minutes. It honestly used to drive me nuts and made me contemplate the pros and cons of leaving the prison they referred to as "Dorm". Looking out the window of my first-floor room, I happened to glimpse a mustard-yellow umbrella blowing out of control in the wind with a young, frustrated girl struggling to keep it in her grasp. She was trying her best not to get her navy blue cardigan and khaki skirt soaked by the downpour, but again, this was Mandeville, so it was a lost cause. After a few moments of struggling, I saw her give up and let the wind waltz with the umbrella, taking it on a trip from which it would never return. But then, she quickly took out a small, pastel-pink umbrella from her leather knapsack and glanced around to see if anyone had witnessed her lose that very entertaining battle with the elements. She spotted me in the window, instantly rosy-ing her cheeks. She looked down quickly at her black shoes in embarrassment. I chuckled to myself as she rushed off.

The pretty, olive-skinned girl, with the doe eyes, petite body and gently sculpted legs. Her hands looked soft from where I was, with her hair slicked back in a tight bun. And, she was radiant on this dreary day. After that, I would see her sparingly around the campus. So naturally, I thought nothing of it, until one day in the cafeteria I saw her in a red, knitted sweater that left me mesmerized. Images of her would vividly flash across my mind while going through the motions of my day. Fast forward to the next few months on that fateful day at the start of the next semester. The first class.

We were packed tightly like sardines within the much-too-small lecture theatre. I was hot and clammy and contemplating ditching this whole affair as I was on the edge of a panic attack which was about to pop in and say 'hello', and I was not having it today.

That's when YOU walked in and sat closer to me, than I had initially realized.

You were so much more beautiful than I'd ever anticipated and honestly, I was caught off guard. I noticed the hazel flecks in your eyes, and I was in awe. Then there were your lips: lips that looked like they were dipped in honey, offering every promise of beauty, pleasure, peace...love. Like you were fashioned by Aphrodite herself. You glanced in my direction, and for a minute, it seemed like you recognized me. I panicked, as I was trying my best to not have any conversations, in case the anxiety tried to slip out. As you were about to say your first words to me, the lecturer walked in, and I was saved by the bell as class began.

2

As a patron of the literary arts, it was with great pleasure that I made my presentation to the class on "Pride and Prejudice," the romantic novel by Jane Austen, for which we were being graded. I am not usually a fan of public speaking, but this one I didn't mind. The story gripped me in ways unimaginable, especially the topsy-turvy relationship between Elizabeth Bennet and Fitzwilliam Darcy. YOU reminded me so much of her: your quick-witted, humorous, sharp tongue which kept me and those around you on our toes like you did in every class discussion. Just like Mr Darcy, I was more cold and aloof than I'd like to admit but for a good reason, as you'd come to learn. I kept my cards close to my chest and only spoke through my creative work. I guess you could say I had a wealth of my own, not in material things, but more so in feelings and how I tried to express myself. So many times I had compared myself to him while reading the book and as my best friend said, they saw me within every single book or movie I suggested for them to explore. Bennet and Darcy, were such an unlikely pairing. But that was only to the reader who wasn't looking closely enough and couldn't relate as we could. Most importantly, they were a match that had the potential to be great…But I digress, as we are talking about YOU, of course. I wonder though…could YOU possibly be my Elizabeth Bennet?

So bewitched was I, that I got caught up in my musings about us. I was unfocused and fumbled through my presentation. I was not pleased with my performance, as it wasn't the best it could have been and I could see that from the way you were looking at me. Sensing that I had done something wrong, I became anxious...again. I really needed to get a firm handle on my emotions as it relates to you. How did you do this to me? Affect me like this? I didn't even know you! But I wanted to. I wanted to talk to you. I really did. I ached with the longing. Like every love song ever sung, I would do unimaginable things to interest you, intrigue you, win you; which was pretty absurd, because I was not in love with you...*I think*? I just had this strong attraction to you and I wanted to please you in every way possible, but I still didn't know you. I didn't even know your name. What was your name?!

The class ended, and naturally, Mandeville's dysfunctional weather drenched the campus with the most dismal downpour; and I had forgotten my umbrella...just my luck. Just then, a tap on my left shoulder caused me to make a startled spin, and there we were, face-to-face, only a few inches between us in the crowded lobby. And I saw you, as if for the first time. I noticed distinct facial features that I had missed from a distance. The prominence of your jawbone struck me: obvious, but not what I expected. Your olive-brown skin complimented it and your doe eyes, they were hazel like sparkling pools of honey that I would do a world-class dive into, receiving perfect tens from the judges. You asked in that soft, sweet voice if I had an umbrella, and I shook my head. So you proceeded to offer me a 'ride' down to the dorm since we were going in the same direction. "Of course", I nodded. I tried to keep it cool, not passing up the opportunity to finally have a much-anticipated conversation with you. The pastel pink umbrella popped out and I smiled to myself remembering the first time I saw you, and together, we walked to the dorm.

※ ※ ※

The energy in every situation is crucial, especially for individuals who make any sort of art and your energy was pure, unmatched and something I had not encountered in a long time. The possibilities buzzed in my veins. We walked and talked and I found out that you majored in Business Management with an emphasis in Marketing. Ambitious really, but your heart was elsewhere; I saw it glinting in your eyes. Business was never your passion; it never made you feel alive! Instead, what your eyes told me was you craved for more, so much more, it made your soul, your very being ache; but we simply walked on.

Lost in conversation, you unveiled yourself to me, with absolute comfort like you'd known me all your life. You found yourself sharing your deepest contemplations to me, and though you were shocked by this, you didn't shy away. We spoke of your upbringing, conservative parents, and sheltered life. You gushed about your siblings and your drive to follow in your parents' business savvy footsteps and make them proud. That's why you were here, undertaking this particular course of study. You delightfully babbled on and on, until you said it. You laid it bare: the same wondrous dream I saw glowing from within you. It was now right in the open and it knocked the wind out of both of us.

You didn't want any of it. You longed to create, not just crunch numbers and you finally admitted it, to yourself and...to me. You stiffened and we paused on the sidewalk, as at that moment, we realized that something had to change and change now. But how would we change a second-year, magna cum laude student, who had spent her all, focusing on business, to a creative whose soul runs freely? Wouldn't that be next to impossible? Till now, you never knew yourself. Not really anyway, but now you did; you had found yourself. And I had found you. I had always prided myself on being able to at least spark a yearning within friends to create more and act on the artistic inclinations that formed in their heads that they were too scared to act upon. You would be no different, but there was no rush. You had me to help you on this journey, and it was my utmost pleasure to walk this road with you side-by-side if you would have me. We had this whole friendship, fresh and new, to help you truly bloom.

As we neared my 'stop', I took in every aspect of this encounter, committing each intricate detail to memory; my memory of YOU. As we parted ways, I remembered that I still didn't know your name. You said something that pulled me from my trance; you simply asked my name and I replied. Then I realized, as you bade me farewell, that what I needed was never to know your name. It was enough instead, to hear mine wafting gently on the breath from your supple lips. The sweetest blessing to take with me till we meet again...

3

I never thought I would be put in a position to tell someone about you. Maybe in the back of my head, I visualized telling our children? I would take them along for the ride telling our love story through every artistic expression available. They would giggle and swoon to hear about a union so true. They would learn from us the steps to courtship and where we may have fumbled, they'd seek to correct. And they would be there to watch the rest of the story unfold. Though I would start at the beginning, they'd learn to know and love you just as much as I do as I would tend to that process with such great care, just as I did at the very beginning, which started with our first date, which in fact my dear, is tonight.

❋ ❋ ❋

I was as nervous as anyone could be for a first date, but why? I wasn't used to these human-romantic-emotion-things and seeing that it was my, well, our first date I wanted it to be next to perfect. I rushed around the confines of my house preparing for this date.

Thursday, 5:00 p.m.
First, a quick shower, then the whirlwind getting-ready process got on its way. I doused myself in the cologne you complimented

me on the first time we talked. You favoured warm colours or at least I was guessing you did since your favourite season is fall, so I reached for my mustard button-down silk shirt. I paired it with a pair of classic black jeans, and completed the ensemble with black Chelsea boots which I remembered you had a fascination with; thankfully I owned a pair. *Maybe we'd end up matching.* I smiled to myself as I reviewed my outfit, and hoped you'd be pleased.

5:45 p.m.
I stepped out of the house at a cool quarter to six and headed to the main road to catch a taxi to the town centre, to stop by the local flower shop first. You grew up planting roses and tulips in your backyard, so I asked the florist to cut me three roses and two tulips. Two roses, a tulip for you and one each for your mom, because remember, first impressions last; and that was my aim with you: to last.

6:00 p.m.
As I walked to the restaurant, I recalled how a week ago I made the reservation and asked specifically to be placed on the balcony so you could see the iridescent sunset beautifully painting the sky, just as we'd be commencing our evening. You told me that as a little girl you would watch the sky as the sun slipped away. Alas, the hectic demands of life had robbed you of those peaceful wondrous moments and you always wished that you could do it again. Then again, of course, that magna cum laude GPA didn't come out of thin air, not that I'm questioning your ability or anything. *Laughs nervously.* But consider this my first gift to you...of many more to come.

6:15 p.m.
Finally, you were here, and at just the right time too. If you came any later, I would have had to pay extra to hold up the sun and a young broke college student only had a finite amount of money, so I'm glad you came when you did. Although I would have done

whatever I needed to do, to ensure that this evening was perfect. Your eyes glimmered in amazement at the calibre of the restaurant, and twinkled at the ambience, as you took it all in. A meek smile broke into a wide grin as you thanked me for the invitation, and I beamed with pride for putting together a stellar evening, as we perused the menus before us.

6:45 p.m.
As dessert rolled around, I ordered a cheesecake wonton draped in maple syrup, rumoured to be your favourite (yes, I did my research). I whispered this to the waitress as she left to fetch our wine and the bill. When she returned with the delicacy, you looked at me with tenderness, and reached for my hand across the table. You gently squeezed. I'd noticed that about you: when you were excited, you got quiet and squeezed whatever your hand was wrapped around. I was glad this time, that it was mine; I thought they fit together perfectly.

7:00 p.m.
At the end of the night, we walked hand-in-hand and you nuzzled close, telling me how special I'd made your night. I asked if there was anything I could've done better; you stopped and turned to face me, gently squeezing my hand once again to reassure me that it was the best night you had ever encountered. I blushed and looked away and we walked on. Then, I stubbed that same Chelsea boot on a stone and fell in the grass. One hell of a night, if you ask me, and we had only just begun.

4

Loyalty. How do you know it's there? Is there some scale or stick by which it can be measured? Some formula of words, actions and choices that when computed, calculate someone's precise loyalty to you? And how do you know if and when to trust someone? What led me to trust you? Was it the pools of honey within your eyes that I so quickly dove into? Was it the sweet tone of your voice that seductively enthralled me in its silky smooth soliloquy? What was it about you that led me to be as loyal as mans' best friend?

In my experience, loyalty is respecting someone to the point where there is trust. Because, if you don't have trust, then what have you got? You don't hurt them. You don't betray them. You don't bring them along a path which would lead to their utter demise, physically, emotionally and every other 'ally' there is and could be.

❋ ❋ ❋

After our date, I enjoyed every waking moment with you, and you with me. Around you, I was different. I was driven to be the best version of myself that I could be around you. You made me into a different man. A better man. A better man...for you.

Trusting has always been a problem for me. Why? Because I had been stabbed in the back countless times for being too nice, too friendly or too whatever else. Going into this, I had faith in you; faith that *YOU* would be different. I mean, you'd proven yourself; hadn't you?

Saturday, October 19th 2019, 7 pm

As I walked home from spending a glorious day with my friends, I got a call. It was you. We chatted for a while and you said you wanted to see me. I agreed to this, collected a few things from my dorm room and made my way to where you were. You greeted me at your dorm door with the warmest embrace and told me that you had plans for us: we were heading off campus to your friend's house. A bit puzzled as to why we needed to go off campus, I didn't argue because mother always said 'happy wife, happy life'. I hailed a taxi and we made our way to the destination. Upon approaching the house, you asked me to stay outside for a bit. At this point, I was thoroughly confused because it wasn't my birthday and we had only just started dating, so I didn't know what to expect; nevertheless, no complaints from me. I let you have your way.

After a few minutes, you emerged from the house, ready to lead me inside blindfolded, for the sake of this surprise you'd been holding at ransom from me. You walked me into the room, removed your hands from my eyes and before me was dinner, wine and our own private movie night, of my favourite film, **Inception**. You remembered! Which was to be expected, due to my countless hours of babbling about the greatness of this movie, even though we had already watched it numerous times in our first few weeks of being together. But somehow, you still found a way to make it even better. I turned to face you with the biggest grin I could muster and pulled you into the tightest bear hug. You proved to me that you listened, you paid attention and you cared.

Here's the catch though: that night mattered way more than you could even fathom, because earlier that day, I'd seen you going about your business. My beautiful queen, I watched you, smitten from a distance, as we both did our own thing. But something unsettled me. I saw you talking to a guy, which was normal. You're very likeable and already had lots of male friends, but I'd hoped never to see you with this one: I KNEW HIM. No matter though, you were free to talk to guys, but there was something about this particular conversation that made me linger a bit longer than I'd intended to. A little uneasy.

It was *how* you were talking to him. You did that thing you only ever did with me: that little giggle, with the coy side-eye. What's more, is that when we'd caught up at the end of the day, you never mentioned that meeting, or at least not until I brought it up. When I did though, you were quick to dispel any confusion about the encounter. You took the time to calm my insecurities, and you reassured me repeatedly that he was just a new friend and I had nothing to worry about. This proved that you actually cared. You wanted me. You wanted us to work. You wanted us to have a future.

YOU proved that you were different from the others and that you would do right by me. YOU were *not* supposed to disappoint me. Why would you do that to me, princess? Why would you even think of HIM?

HE was everything I was not.

Model individual, head of the class, choir director, spiritually-inclined, right wing conservative, just like your parents. The whole works. He dabbled in the technical part of media, dipping his toes into photography and audio-engineering. He even graced the keys of the piano every now and then, elegantly making them succumb to his touch. HE was like me, but not. Because HE didn't see you the way I did. And you didn't see HIM the way I did; no one saw HIM the way I did. Everyone has a dark side; I wish you had seen his. Or, I at least wish you had waited.

※ ※ ※

I noticed the changes in you two months before things went down: you joined the choir; we were talking less and frankly, you were spending all of your time with HIM. And you didn't even realize it, but I did. I noticed the little things: the strained conversations, the awkward interactions, the tension, the distance. I felt it. I felt further from you. I felt like a stranger with memories that would hauntingly replay in my head each night; and with all this, as your boyfriend, I still had faith that maybe this was a phase, or was this a way to prove to your parents that you could end up with the "guy" they always hoped you would? Was this their doing? Your parents? Because when I met them, I never felt welcomed in their presence. I could tell that they wished you had chosen someone else: someone more like you. Maybe they wanted you to choose him.

I remember the brunch that almost cost us everything. Looking across the table at your face and all we had been through, who would have really thought that this would've been that day. Life is pretty crazy, right?

There we were, facing each other on either side of the salad, looking at the feast set before us. We grew up in similar homes with similar value systems but we both took different approaches in our views about life. You, the 'conventional traditional' and me, 'the artistic visionary'.

Enter your parents: Traditional Conservatives, firm in their belief that children should follow stringent guidelines within the realm of their religious upbringing and should work within the realm of the church. I've always been opposed to conforming to 'the system', whatever system it might be. They wanted you to be a part of *that* system: the system HE was a part of, the system I abhorred. And you, my dear, were on the fringe of that system, teetering on the fine line, unsure of where to give your soul.

Lunch that day was tense. I steadied my hands as I passed the beans to my right and received the pasta from my left, all the while my legs shook beneath the surface of the table cloth. Every question seemed less like a calm 'getting to know you' and more like a condescending investigative judgement. I answered between bites as best as I could, trying to find the right things to say while still being true to myself. I tried to speak with respect but also confidence as your parents cross-examined me. They never broke a sweat, as they daintily cut their meal with their knives and forks and sly scrutiny across their brows.

Your parents made it very clear that they detested my choice to 'be rebellious' and frowned upon the fact that I had the support of my own parents, fellow Conservatives. They disapproved of the fact that my parents allowed me to move off of the dorm and live by myself. They considered me to be a young naive boy who knew nothing of the world and had nothing to offer their little princess.

On the flip side, they loved HIM. HE was what they envisioned when they retired to their bed at night and thought of their future as grandparents and the honourable young man they'd give you away to. I had hoped this wasn't the case and was just my fears playing on my mind, but I got my confirmation on another weekend, not too long after.

The choir HE had convinced you to join was invited to sing at a worship service near to your home church. I accompanied you to this performance, and there, we encountered your parents again as they had decided to swing by to see you. The interaction was strained, but I had anticipated it and did my best to stay afloat while your parents took subtle jabs at me. Then, HE strolled up wanting to borrow you for a quick rehearsal of your solo, and for a split second, the tension wafted away with HIS brisk witty introduction. Your parents' eyes twinkled as they shared some light banter with HIM, and as quickly as the pressure had eased, it returned, as they looked at me with disdain. HE was what they wanted for their little girl, their baby girl...my baby girl. They wanted HIM.

*** * ***

On that fateful day, in the midst of a thunderous downpour, you said you wanted to talk. I had been dreading this day for weeks, and I had tried my best to avoid it. I had taken you to all your favourite places and we had done so many of your favourite things. I had done my utmost to make you happy, keep you happy. During this ominous talk, you recounted that you'd met someone. You'd been seeing HIM for a while. Your parents seemed to like HIM; HE was exactly the son-in-law they'd always envisioned for their precious daughter. For you.

You spouted that rehearsed, well-intentioned rhetoric about how much I meant to you and that you didn't want things to change between us; but they already had, as you weren't present anymore. When you were physically with me, your mind was elsewhere. With HIM. That was the choice you made, and with that, I knew we were through. Not because you wanted *us* to be through, but simply because if not, your precious relationship with your parents might be shattered. I mean, choosing HIM was the easy way out. The simple solution. They saw me as your downfall and feared that you would follow in my footsteps straight to perdition. They caused you constant grief about us, but with HIM, you'd have no unrest. All would be well in their world, the world you were choosing to stay sheltered in to prove your loyalty to them. And you most certainly did... but at my expense.

5

I NSOLENT.

    adjective. Showing a rude and arrogant lack of respect.

And insolent is what HE was. Is.

At times, I sit back and think about how vastly different things could be if we made amends. If you'd listened to me. If you'd just waited and let the phase pass or if HE had never been in the picture at all. Because we were good together. You know we were. But you still chose to go. Then again, you didn't know HIM like I did. So this is where I tell you my side of the story. My story of HIM.

Growing up, attending the same school, the same church, our parents being friends since before our births, we were destined to be friends and that's what we became. We were best friends. No, we were brothers. Being the only children for both our parents, it was the closest we came to having actual biological siblings. We were a dynamic duo like all the greats: Batman and Robin, Shaggy and Scooby-Doo, Spongebob and Patrick. We were inseparable! No one came between us. But soon, time did. School did. Life did. On different paths, we drifted further and further apart. His family moved to the other end of the island and we would only see each other occasionally…if that much. I missed my brother. I really missed HIM. Five years passed. I'd heard from my mother that he'd changed, but changed how? Was he taller? More focused? Was his hair longer? Bro, are you married? Wait...that wouldn't make sense. (That's what happens when I get ahead of myself).

I received a call one morning from his mother's number. Having not spoken to her in a long time, I slid the receiver to answer her, but it was...HIM. Naturally, I was shocked, since it was the first since I'd heard his voice in so long. But then we began to talk fluidly like I just saw HIM yesterday. We talked for hours, catching up on past events, major and minor achievements... like brothers all over again. HE mentioned heading to university, and out of curiosity, I asked which one? It was the one I was attending. HE said it was going to be just like when we were growing up. What?! You mean "the good ole' days"? Of your abuse? Your impudence? Sweeping the girls I had or wanted from out of my grasp? Ridiculing me in front of crowds of friends and strangers alike?

As I said, I missed my bro, but time and space had made me realize some less than desirable traits about him. Being away from him all this time, I realized that he hadn't been such a "good" person back then. Maybe it was because we were kids and hadn't found ourselves yet and just didn't know any better. Or maybe, that's just who he was. Either way, in retrospect, I'd come to believe that maybe our growing apart had been in my best interest.

If he was anything like before, then I was suddenly not excited for him to be around. Actually, I'd take a "hard pass" on that. He was rude, arrogant, had no regard for any authority figure and treated everyone as if they were beneath him. Not to mention that he was disrespectful and just plain mean to any girl who made the sorry mistake of even giving him the time of day...and I let him get away with it back then, because...well, I don't know why. But I didn't stop him then. But that wouldn't be the case now. That's why I didn't want HIM to know you existed; but HE seemed so different, better, more respectable.

Operative word: *SEEMED.*

But I miscalculated. Misjudged. <u>My mistake</u>.

The part of him that I knew, the part that defined who he was, was not the part he showed to you. I guess those drama classes he used to take didn't go to waste. He embodied the perfect boy that any girl would want to take home to their parents, but I didn't. I could be, but I chose not to be. And due to my bad luck, HE chose the girl I had. It had to be the girl I had. It had to be YOU. I tried warning you about HIM. About his insolence. About how and who he truly was...is. But you were convinced that I was just jealous because you were leaving me for HIM. You thought I was the insolent one, but I wasn't...I promise you. I just saw the destruction ahead.

6

At first, seeing you together wasn't as bad as I thought it would be. I would say 'hi', and you would politely reply when he was around. Then, when we were alone, you'd be all over me and in my arms. You left me conflicted. Was it the 'rush' that you enjoyed with me? The idea that we could possibly get caught? The recklessness of it all? Did I finally make you feel alive? I think that's what made me attractive to you. The classic mistake of you loving your idea of me, as opposed to loving me for who I really was. I made it appear that I had no direction for my life. To you, I represented freedom; rebellion even. A chance at another path, yet to be forged, that you had the chance to chart. You were happy to throw caution to the wind with me. All of the commitment but none of it at the same time.

But that's where you were wrong, my dear. I had a clear direction. I had a plan. I knew where I wanted to go and who I wanted to go with. It makes me wonder if those deep conversations had just rolled right off your back and passed you by. The ones about where we saw ourselves in 5 and 10 years. The talks about future ambitions and how we'd get there, both together and apart. Those questions about kid's names and parenting styles. Those stories and lessons of and from our own upbringings. It's like they were all void of value. I saw my future, with you in it. But it was misunderstood. I was misunderstood…especially by the person who I thought would understand me the most…you.

Originally, I thought this was you trying something new. Then you'd come back to me, missing the simultaneous exhilaration and peace of all that we had. But something about him made you stay; maybe the perfection? I couldn't quite put my finger on it. One thing that was for sure: your mother absolutely adored him. So much so that she even stopped asking about me. Like I ceased to exist from the face of the earth. (I oh-so loved her homemade cookies.)

I think seeing you together over and over again though, was harder than I anticipated it would be because you seemed happy, or happier than you were when you had been with me. Had I not done all that I could've? Did I not give you the earth, moon and stars? Was it not enough for you? See? We always knew, you never could be satisfied.

Then it happened. A rainy day in the month of November; I received a phone call and you were crying. Did the gods above see that you were devastated and decide to make the weather reflective of your state? I listened to your pained story.

"We had a fight."

"About?"

"Some girl I saw him texting."

"You went through his phone?"

"Yea..."

"Why?"
"Because I don't think I'm the only one."

"So, do you think he's cheating on you with this other girl?"

"Yup, and I don't want to hear 'I told you so'."

"I mean, I did tell you."

" Doesn't mean you have to rub it in that I was wrong."

" I'll take the opportunity because it is honestly a rare occurrence."

" I hate you!"

"Only because you know how right I am and that I warned you that this would happen."

"Twice in one day? You're on a roll, hun."

"HuN? Is this you finally coming to your senses about me?"

"YOU are not the one. I appreciate you but YOU're not for me. Goodbye"

And as quickly as it started, it ended. I didn't know what to make of it. I believe that she missed me but maybe, just then, I'd fumbled my chance. It seemed that our ship had sailed.

Seeing him do the same thing I warned you about disappointed me. I thought that for you he would be different or at least feel guilty about his actions and change for the better?

Conversations between the both of you appeared (from where I stood) heavily one-sided: you didn't seem to have a voice; He overpowered you with everything. Your opinions? Gone. Your ideas? Nonexistent. Your hopes and dreams? To be modelled after his. You were not his partner, his girlfriend, his best friend. You weren't even a person to him. You were a 'trophy girl'. You looked good on his arm and were good for his ego. You were something that he only wanted to know he owned and boasted about. Someone, he didn't know how to treat well. A slave of sorts, in his head.

But this wasn't just my biased opinion or observation: Unbeknownst to the both of you, mutual friends would come to me with concerns about you and him. They'd say how he was behaving, and how he didn't value you and wasn't right for you. They suggested I talk to him and try to give him some perspective since he used to be my friend before all of this. As usual, I disagreed but over time, I caved because...why wouldn't I? I loved you.

7

It should be noted that I'm not a confrontational person, but I knew HIM and since we had a history, I figured he would listen to me as a bro. I happened to come across him when he was with you and instantly thought that this was a terrible idea, but did he know how he made you feel? His constant condescension didn't imply that he did, so I was gonna make sure that he knew.

You should remember this day quite well.

My plan was simple: tell him that he is hurting you and that he should leave, because he certainly wasn't gonna do better. I mean, I knew him. It wasn't rocket science, right? So I approached you both, greeted you, and asked if I could have a quick chat with him alone. He said,

"Anything you want to say to me, you can say in front of my girl!"

This damned idiot.

"I think you need to break up with HER."

You looked up instantly in horror and I **knew** that this was the worst idea in the history of bad ideas.

"What did you just say, bro?"

Did he really just call me 'bro'? Now I know he heard what I said, so you would wonder why he would need me to repeat myself, but for love, we do absurd and crazy things.

"I strongly suggest that you break up with HER."

I was not about to *tell* him what to do; it was merely a friendly suggestion.

"And leave her to be happy without you."

Then I walked off, because who was I to tell this man what to do with his girlfriend. Wasn't it *his* relationship?

Later that night, you thanked me for coming to your rescue. You said that even though you were mortified, you could clearly see how hard that was for me. I chuckled and said that it was nothing, even though we both knew otherwise. I tried to play it cool but I couldn't hold it in any longer; I asked if you'd finally split. Your response? You were both happier than ever...together.
My. Heart. Dropped.

8

So, sickness is the state of being ill. Was I ill? Were you the sickness I couldn't avoid? Couldn't recover from? There are some illnesses like that seasonal common cold you always catch no matter how careful you are, that you just can't shake. She was my prime example, and trust me, I was down for the count.

Day 1

It'd been 3 weeks since we last talked. I got home with a headache. I thought nothing of it because I'd had a long and stressful day and I probably just needed some rest. I'd lost my appetite so I went straight to bed, but I woke up with my head pounding. I reasoned that it was because I hadn't eaten anything the night before, but my appetite was still gone. So, I shrugged it off and got on with my day.

Day 2

I staggered to my door, mind racing through all those times I took not feeling like this for granted. I barely made it inside and decided to prepare a meal to the best of my abilities. That is a miserably failed attempt as I find myself preparing a meal that we once shared. Hey! Food is food. A guy's gotta eat and I was not gonna stop eating a certain thing because it reminded me of you. But what is wrong with me? Why did I feel like this? What was happening? All I knew is that I hated this feeling. I hated this sick feeling growing in my stomach...and it finally made sense why: I was in withdrawal.

But could you be in withdrawal from *someone*? No, it couldn't be! Could you crave them so much that you desired for them to be in your life no matter the consequences? That didn't make logical sense, but were you the reason I couldn't function? The bug I caught, was it you? Were you my love bug? Get it? Cause bugs make you sick?

Why did I have to be in love with you? Why did I have to get sick because of you? Because is this how it felt to be without you? I hated this feeling. You took my heart and shattered it into a million pieces, yet here I am again trying to love you with each and every individual splinter...three weeks after you left me! Mark you, the wounds were still fresh but I shouldn't be sick! A whole sickness?! This was an infeasible connotation of my human mind. For once in my life, I had no idea what to do. You left me speechless. Helpless and in a weakened state; my body aching to be better. I knew that I had to get over you but I didn't know how or even where to start.

The worst part about all of this was that you seemed to be doing fine without me. The pristine pinnacle of health. While I was here, struggling to keep my head above water. Struggling to keep sane. To survive whatever this was. Did you know that you had done this to me? Was this HIS idea? Did HE put you up to this? Was this some sort of sick revenge plot for something I did years ago? Not only was I sick unto death, but I was also conjuring up conspiracy theories about both of you.

You were the light of my world, the healer in my life, *music note* the Tylenol I would take when my head hurt, my water that could quench my thirst if I were stuck in the desert *music note*.

This is why I was deathly bedridden. Sick to my core...or at least I thought I was sick. Let's check: Fever? Fatigue? Feelings of missing you? Yup, yup and yup. Well if it waddles like a duck and quacks like a duck, it can't be a fish.

Could this have truly been avoided though? There was no prescribed drug that could have healed me at that moment. No home remedies I could've fallen back on. I had to 'tough it out'. This was an unavoidable sickness. My 'almost descent' into madness. Madness without, no, because of...YOU.

9

(The madness and how I overcame it)

* * *

After my illness, I was a different person. A new man, so to speak. I realized that what I experienced couldn't have been avoided when it came to you. You were the best experience of my first year of university life and I thank you for that. You changed me into a person who was more compassionate, more caring, more appreciative.

When I met you, I was manipulative, vengeful and would have done anything to keep you with me, to make sure that you never left. I would've given you ultimatums that would make you reconsider your love for me and how great it was and could be. I was toxic and thought I had no right to be in a committed and loving relationship. I never deserved the love you gave me because it was too raw and it was too pure, but it was exactly what I needed to make me better.

I indulged in it and dove right in. It was new to me, refreshing, genuine and innocent, similar to a newborn child not privy to the evils that it would encounter growing up in this cold, harsh, perverted world. All you wanted to do was nurture it and keep it safe and close. You and our love had been that for me. My mannerisms began to change vastly: I listened more, tried to communicate effectively and I was truthful, almost to a fault. I trusted you and didn't manipulate. I made sure to allow myself to be vulnerable with and to you. I made sure you felt secure in our relationship and wouldn't be concerned that I was being unfaithful or making you look like a fool. I'd been told plenty of times before that love changes you. I was excited about the changes I began to see and feel within myself after you entered my life. Who would have thought that I would've gotten here?

My family commented on the newfound twinkle they saw in my eyes, a twinkle that you gave me. A twinkle that was solely dependent on you, which turned out to be bad for my health when you left, but with your absence I grew. I learnt more about myself. But more than that, I was able to really face myself and reconcile my flaws. I saw what I had done and how I could be better as a person and began that hard work on myself during my "illness".

Going into that sickness with all that rage, all those dark thoughts of the betrayal that I thought I had received, was a dark painful journey, but it shaped me into someone who was the best version of himself...or was at least on his way to knowing who that person was and how to get to him. You helped me to emerge into and bask in the light, ready to shower it onto the next person I would love and seek to give my all. To love them purely and without conditions or bounds. To trust them wholeheartedly and have full transparency with them. You made me and my love stronger.

To understand who I am now would be to understand where I am coming from, what I went through and where I am now. You see?

That's the thing. I never really got over YOU. I soared to mountain tops with you and crawled through valleys with you. You brought me euphoric ecstasy. My experiences lived with you are ones that I will never forget, I mean, who could forget those? Who would want to? I will have a love for you until the end of time, regardless of how we ended and I am forever grateful to you for sharing your pastel pink umbrella with me on that short but monumental walk to my dormitory. My journey is one that I am thankful for, and I'm blessed to have shared even a small part of it with you. I will forever love YOU, for this is who I truly am: Yours. Forever and always.

10

Even though change is often difficult, many times it's also for the best, or at least that's what I've learned to tell myself and so far it works in getting me through my days. The right kind of change pushes us beyond our comfort zones and that's what you did for me. Going after you was different because YOU were different. It was new, exhilarating and single-handedly one of the best moments of my life…everything considered. And it all started when I heard my name wafting gently on the breath from your supple lips.

Do you know that question people love to ask that goes:

> *"if you could go back to a particular moment in your past with your current knowledge, which one would you choose and is there anything you would change or do differently?"*

I think about that a lot when it comes to us. You still invade my thoughts, capture my mind and arrest me so profoundly, even after all this time. I'm past the hurt of our whole situation, and as I said, I've grown from it. But it's all fine and dandy until I'm out for a night with friends, and these deep, existential questions come up when the good food has settled in our stomachs and the 'food coma' is about to knock us out for the count.

THE STORY OF HER

I believe that everyone has to change. Everyone is subject to change because as human beings, we should be growing and evolving in each aspect of our lives, and that fateful day when we walked to the dorm was when my life began to change, and this change involved you. Amusingly all of this started when I saw you through my window and you ended up in my class and on both occasions, the weather was doing the most. Isn't that curious? Or could that be a universal sign that I was meant to talk to you and you were meant to change my life?

So this is my answer to that question and how I would relive that day when I embraced change. This is how I will remember you, and it and us, because the irony is...I wouldn't change a thing.

* * *

I always dreamt that we'd tell this story to our kids one day, about how mom and dad met on a rainy day, and it flourished into something beautiful. But that would be hard to do if I didn't remember your name and at this moment it's evading me, which is hilarious because here I am formulating plans for our future.

In Greek mythology, the story is told of Aphrodite, the goddess of love: a beautiful woman often accompanied by the winged godling Eros, who was birthed by rising from the sea foam. Your name, I'm sure, was crafted by Aphrodite herself and I should be eternally damned by the gods for forgetting it. What I vividly remember though, are the cool winds of Manchester coupled with the scantily clad sky, that had the workings of a beautiful day, which it was because it is when I see you again for the first time in a few weeks after our fateful walk to the dorm.

Sitting at a gazebo conceptualizing a design for my portfolio, you approach me and I smell the delicately tantalizing perfume that faintly dampens your blouse, as I look up to meet your eyes. You remind me of your name, that sweet sweet name that intrigues me. It's interesting; I discovered that it means you are strong in material matters, determined and stubborn. This seems to justify your futile fight with the mustard yellow umbrella that the wind stole when I first laid eyes on you. Maybe it's also where your good business ability stems from? Knowing when to "hold 'em and fold 'em"? Your major makes sense. Creative and outgoing as well? There it is. I knew I wasn't wrong. So many things about YOU just made sense as we sat there and talked about my portfolio for a while, calm and easy like the hilltop breeze that washed us. I felt like I knew you even more than before. I mentioned wanting to turn my project into something profitable, and an action plan was laid out seamlessly by your business sensibility in a matter of minutes. Amazed and in awe, I marvelled at all the truths held in the name with which you were bestowed with such care.

But, I wonder if you think this way about me?

Are you musing about me as I reveal myself to you, a treat so rare you don't even realize?

Seeing you gush over my artistic ability was heartwarming and endearing. I offered to teach you to draw, paint and see photography as isolated moments in time; and as simple as it seemed, you were elated by this idea, especially the chance to do it with me.

Other students moved around us going about their business, but we are locked in a bubble of just us. We continued our conversation so fluidly, time escaped us under that gazebo. At the end of that day, I realized just as I did in the beginning, that the work you'd take would be difficult, foreign even; but I greeted it as an unknown adventure which I'd heartily embark on without hesitation. I thought to myself that one day it may take us to vast cities and extraordinary islands. We would dance in the streets to the strum of a Spanish guitar in the pale moonlight, and no, I don't mean that symbolically or metaphorically. For I saw potential and purpose and a story unwritten in your honey-coloured eyes.

❊ ❊ ❊

And even now, it is the greatest story I could ever wish to tell. Maybe not to our children, maybe not to anyone, maybe just to YOU...But it is one I cherish with all I have. The story of YOU, my HER, from then until now I hold you in my heart...and what a wonderful story YOU are.

EPILOGUE

If God ever came down and asked me what my biggest regret in my life was, I would say it was choosing the wrong person to fall in love with.

Notice I said *choosing,* because the truth is, I'd already fallen in love. I knew it with every fibre of my being. I was happy. I was full. Yet still, I made another choice. I let myself be swayed by shiny promises and sweet nothings, and perfect, hollow shadows of something I already had and threw away. And now…

That day, that rainy day, I should have known that he was the one. But as humans, we make mistakes, this being my biggest one…ever. Because I didn't just lose love, I lost all the joy and beauty it afforded. I lost the chance to be the real me.

Now, conforming to this life with HIM is my rightful sentence, and as such, I will carry my cross.

If I had the chance to fix it, I would. Just another opportunity to choose, I wouldn't be so naive. I was wrong. I'm sorry. I will forever love…YOU.

Wait! Could it be? Is it really happening? Do you mean it might not be too late?

ACKNOWLEDGEMENTS

Big up my teacher, Mrs Popsaan Francis, for allowing me to write about one consistent topic for the whole semester; that's how this whole thing started, and I appreciate her for that.

I want to thank my mom, Raylene Ross, for always believing in me and pushing me to go for my dreams.

Leslie-Ann Lyons, for being there for me.

Ayanna Lewis, for always appreciating my work.

Thank you to that lady at church who said I wouldn't turn out to be anything in life. Hold dis!

Big up my best friend, Karyn Allen. She's been my partner on this project, working with me side-by-side from start to finish, and this book is as much hers as it is mine.

And lastly, I want to thank God for giving me the ability to write this beautiful story for HER.

ABOUT THE AUTHOR

Zachary Ross

An all-rounded creative and general 'art-enthusiast', Zachary Ross is a man of many gifts. Having dabbled in many creative areas, he currently specializes in photography and videography (@wildshotta on Instagram). Ross is also the co-founder of Bere Wildness Productions, a budding production company derived from his YouTube Channel and Podcast, which he does with his best friend Karyn Allen. He is currently a student at the Northern Caribbean University where he is pursuing a Bachelor of Arts Degree in Communication Studies, with an emphasis in Television Production.

Having a love of words from an early age and being blessed with a quick wit and a silver tongue, Ross has always appreciated a good story. With aspirations to be a compelling storyteller, he has taken to this new medium to bring readers a captivating fictional tale sprinkled with non-fictional personal elements. The Story of HER realizes a lifelong dream as his debut novel and the first of three parts to this heartfelt narrative.

Made in United States
Orlando, FL
16 November 2021